This Little Tiger book belongs to:

_____

_____

_____

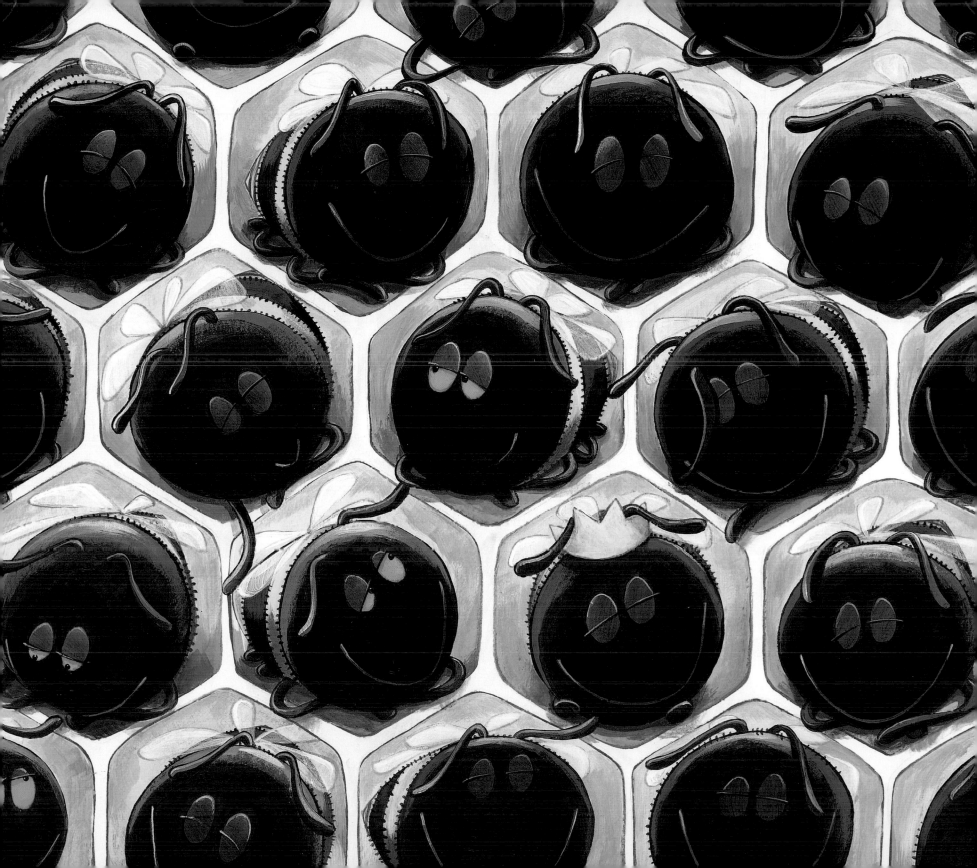

For Sam, who taught me
everything I know about bees
~ S S

For my BEEootiful
BaBEE, Levi
~ J T

LITTLE TIGER PRESS
1 The Coda Centre, 189 Munster Road,
London SW6 6AW
www.littletiger.co.uk

First published in Great Britain 2007
This edition published 2016

Text copyright © Steve Smallman 2007
Illustrations copyright © Jack Tickle 2007
Visit Jack Tickle at www.ChapmanandWarnes.com
Steve Smallman and Jack Tickle have asserted
their rights to be identified as the author and
illustrator of this work under the Copyright,
Designs and Patents Act, 1988
ISBN 978-1-84869-383-8

Printed in China

LTP/1900/1511/0416

10 9 8 7 6 5 4 3 2 1

The Very

Greedy Bee

Steve Smallman   Jack Tickle

LITTLE TIGER PRESS
London

In a busy, buzzy beehive lived a very greedy bee.
All the other bees worked hard making honey
and cleaning the hive, but the Greedy Bee spent
all day gobbling pollen and guzzling nectar.

SLURP! SLURP! BURP!

Eeek!

The Greedy Bee wouldn't share
his nectar with anyone.
He wouldn't even let a tired
ladybird sit on his flower.
   "Find your own flower!" he
shouted. "This one is MINE!"

And when, one day, the Greedy Bee found a meadow full of the biggest, juiciest flowers he had ever seen, he decided not to tell **ANYONE!**

"**YUMMY!**" he buzzed. "Lots and lots of flowers and they're all for **ME!**"

The Greedy Bee whizzed
and bizzed from flower
to flower, slurping and
burping, and growing
FATTER ...

and **FATTER** ...

and **FATTER**...

and **FATTER!**

At last his tummy
was full and he settled
down on a big pink
flower in the warm
yellow sunshine and
fell fast asleep.

z z z z z z z z z z !

When the Greedy Bee woke up,
it was **DARK**. He tried to fly,
but his tummy was so stodgy
and podgy that . . .

he went down instead
of up and landed,
BIFF! BANG! THUMP!
on the ground below.

"I'M SCARED!" cried the Greedy Bee,

"and I don't know how to get home!"

Then he saw two glowing eyes in the long grass.

"EEK!" he cried. "A MONSTER is coming to eat me!"

But it wasn't a monster, it was two friendly
fireflies, their bottoms glowing in the dark.
"What's wrong?" they asked.
"I'm too full to fly," wailed the Greedy Bee,
"and I can't walk home in the dark!"

"Follow us," said the fireflies, and they
all set off on the long, long journey home.

Through forests
of flowers and
squelchy mud . . .

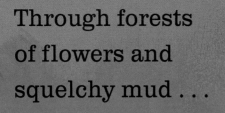

over hills and under
hollows trudged the
Greedy Bee. He had
never walked so far
and he was very tired.

"Soon be there!" called the fireflies kindly.

Then they heard a whooshing, watery noise . . .

"Ha ha! I'm almost home!" cried the
Greedy Bee excitedly. "It's the stream!"
And it was, but his hive was on
the other side of it.

"Oh dear," cried the Greedy Bee, flopping down with a flump on the floor. "How will I ever get across?" he sniffled sadly.

"We'll help you!" said a tiny ant with a big leaf.

The ant and his friends flipped
one of their leaves into the water.
    "Jump in!" they cried.
Then, helped by the fireflies,
the Greedy Bee and the ants
made their way, splishing and
splashing, over to the other side
of the stream.

"**HOORAY, I'M HOME!**" cried the Greedy Bee. "Wherever have you been?" called the other bees. "**I OVERSLURPED!**" said the Greedy Bee. "I would never have got home if my new friends hadn't been so kind, so now I'm going to share my best honey with them. Would you like some too?"

"Great!" said the other bees. "Let's have a party!"

Everyone tucked
into a midnight feast of
yummy, runny honey.
All except for one **VERY**
sleepy, **VERY** happy,
but **NOT** so greedy bee!

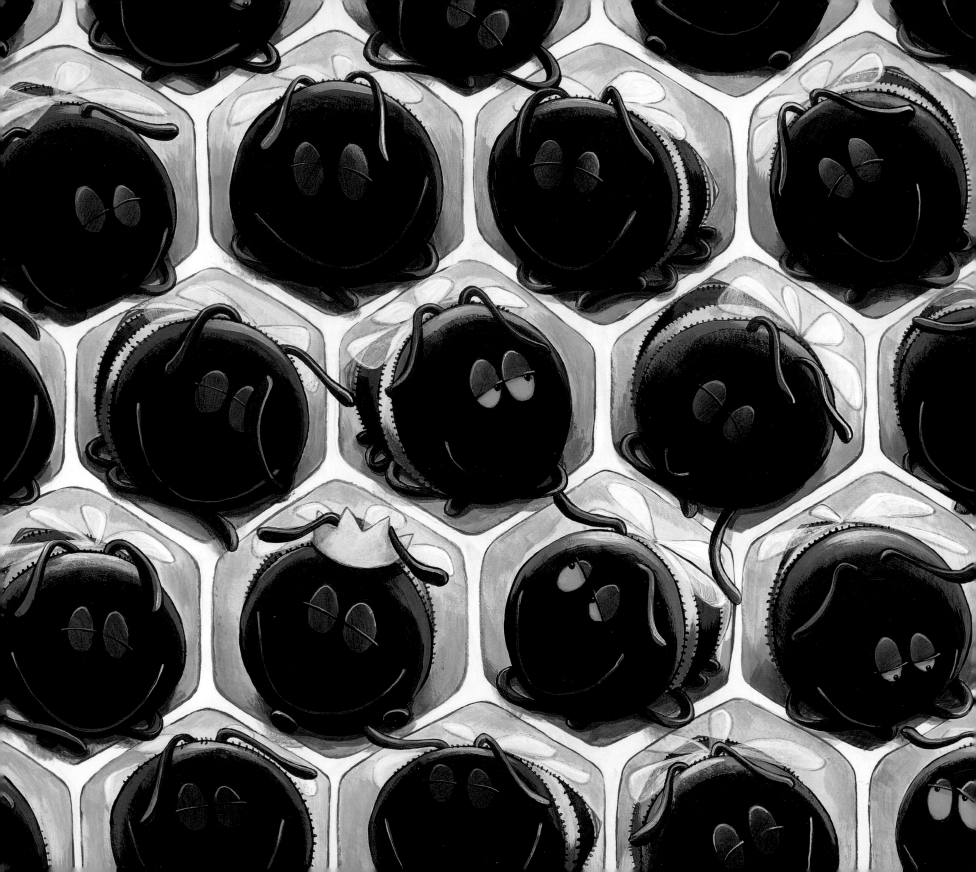

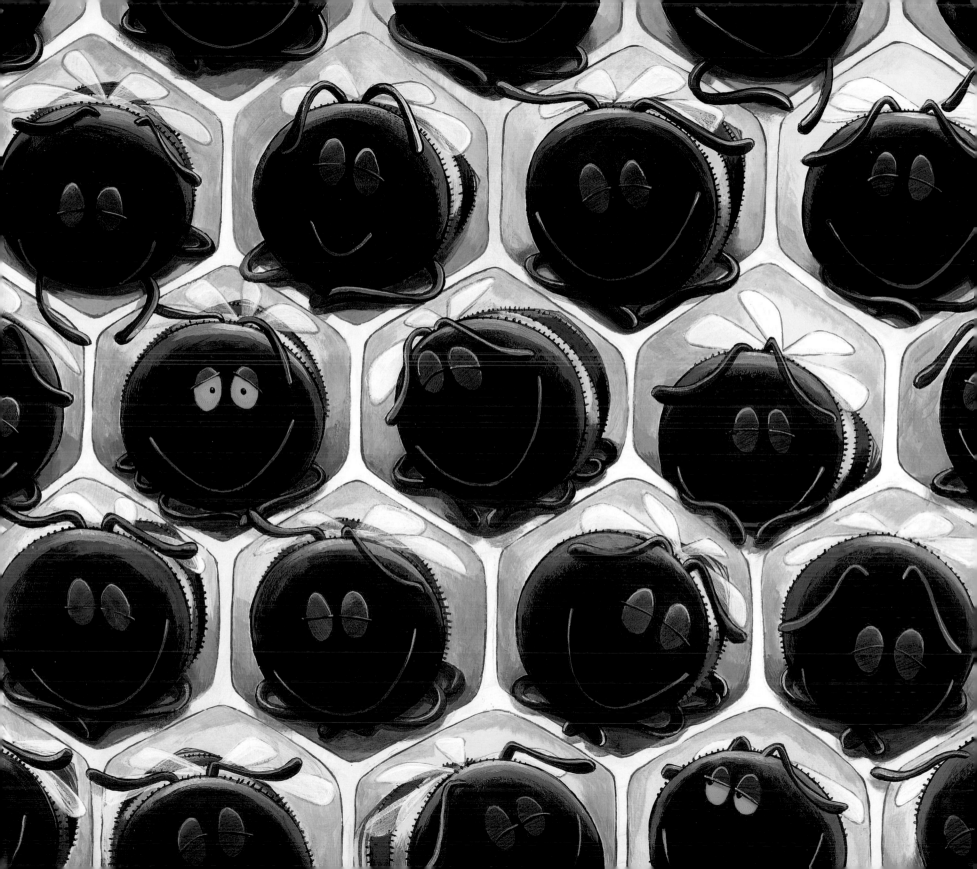

CD track 1 – complete story with original music and sound effects
CD track 2 – story with page turn pings encourages learner readers to join in

Running time – over 15 mins • Produced by Stationhouse • Music composed by Sam Park
Text copyright © Steve Smallman 2007 • This recording copyright © Little Tiger Press 2012

Visit our website www.littletiger.co.uk for details of other Little Tiger Picture
Book and CD Sets, plus our full catalogue of novelty, board and picture books.